Ellie gasped as a second wave of cats came out from the trees, not in ones and twos but thickly, in the kind of numbers you never saw cats, never in the world – in more than tens, more than dozens – in hundreds. Seen in such numbers they seemed in a sense to be more than the sum of themselves, more than simply cats. They seemed a single, purposeful entity.

Ellie strained to number them, however roughly, but could not. They tumbled out now, grey, tabby, black and auburn, and here and there was the pale flash of a head or paw.

'Hundreds!' she guessed. Then, 'Thousands!'

Still they came.

For the hagwitch has begun her attack and, as this enthralling fantasy unfolds, she tries to lure Ellie to her, knowing that her power will be complete once she has the girl in her grasp . . .

Ellie and The Hagwitch

Helen Cresswell
Illustrated by Jonathon Heap

CORGI

ELLIE AND THE HAGWITCH

A CORGI BOOK   0 552 52411 5

Originally published in Great Britain in 1984 by
Patrick Hardy Books

PRINTING HISTORY
Corgi edition published 1987
Corgi edition reprinted 1988, 1989

This book is set in 12/14 pt Century Schoolbook
by Colset Private Limited, Singapore.

Corgi Books are published by Transworld Publishers Ltd.,
61–63 Uxbridge Road, Ealing, London W5 5SA,
in Australia by Transworld Publishers (Australia) Pty. Ltd.,
15–23 Helles Avenue, Moorebank, NSW 2170, and in New
Zealand by Transworld Publishers (N.Z.) Ltd., Cnr. Moselle
and Waipareira Avenues, Henderson, Auckland.

Reproduced, printed and bound in Great Britain by
Hazell Watson & Viney Limited
Member of BPCC plc
Aylesbury, Bucks, England

For Edna with love

Ellie and The Hagwitch

Chapter One

The Braille Wood was the home of the cats, and they came out now, at nightfall. The first few slipped out, swung like shadows. They came with long, low-bellied strides and scarcely moved the grasses. The sun had left all but the tips of the world. It lay in floods here and there and distracted the eye. Only one who was actually watching for the cats would have noticed them as they slid out from the real dark of the wood.

Ellie Barker *was* watching, and now, at the first glimpse of movement, stiffened. She was stiff already. She had been there crouching behind the maythorn for an hour or more, and had felt the dew come and watched the sun fall, and had almost given up.

'It's true, then!'

She gasped as a second wave of cats came out from the trees, not in ones and twos but thickly, in the kind of numbers you never saw cats, never in the world – in more than tens, more than dozens – in hundreds. Seen in such numbers they seemed in a sense to be more than the sum of themselves, more than simply cats. They seemed a single, purposeful entity.

Ellie strained to number them, however roughly, but could not. They tumbled out now, grey, tabby, black and auburn, and here and there was the pale flash of a head or paw.

'Hundreds!' she guessed. Then, 'Thousands!'

Still they came.

'What – what if they never stop coming? What if they come and come and come and fill the field and then the next and come and come, right to our house?'

The vision of sighting the cats in the roadway, of them advancing like an army into the street and past the houses was:

'Impossible!' she decided, watching the impossible cats.

She was wondering now how it would feel to be among them, to be surrounded

by so much fur, so dense a cat crowd. You could put out both hands, she thought, and stroke with both of them at once, and then all the cats would come, purring and rubbing, and the purrs, she imagined, would make a kind of music, quite loud, a sound that had never been heard in the world before. And having thought this, she was at once filled with an intense desire to *hear* a thousand cats – or two thousand, or three – all purring together, to *know* what the sound would be like, for she could not imagine it.

On the other hand, 'I'd be scared!' she admitted to herself, and changed her position a little behind the maythorn, and felt her legs cramped and her knees wet. She watched as the cats patterned the meadow, wove their paths as if making invisible tapestry.

'Why are they coming?' she wondered. 'No *milk* for them – nothing at all, really. More to eat in the wood – rats, mice, birds. . . .'

Very faintly she could hear the river rushing over the stones of the weir beyond the wood.

'Fish? Get fish out the river, could they?'

But the cats were not hunting food here in the meadow, she felt sure of it. And so it was the more mysterious that they should have emerged from the wood at all, and now be pacing the meadow in the fading light, their coats dampened by dew. Ellie had watched for so long now that she began to feel dizzy, tranced.

'Weaving a spell, could they be?'

She reminded herself that she did not believe in spells, or any such things. She strained into the half light for clues, but saw only cats, dense and undulating, and doing nothing and going nowhere, but –

'Me!' she gasped. 'They know I'm here! They're doing it for me!'

What was it the toll keeper had said?

'You watch and you wait and you watch and you wait long enough, and it'll come. Sure as night and certain as day – something'll come.'

She drew a long, shuddering breath and was all at once aware of the loneliness of the meadow and the fast fading of the light, the closing of daisies, and she was terrified and squeezed her eyes tight shut as the only way to escape she could think of.

'Let them go away, let them go away!' she gabbled to herself. And, 'I don't want them, I don't!'

Still she crouched, eyes still fast shut.

She heard only the hissing water beyond the wood and the occasional whistle of a bird. She stayed thus for what seemed a very long time. She was hoping that those stalking cats might suddenly cease to be there if she shut them out and refused to look at them.

'Mustn't even think about them,' she told herself, and fiercely forced herself to forget them, not even imagine they were still there.

'What's for supper? Kippers? No, had them yesterday – lovely, delicious, yum-yum! I *love* kippers and sausages nice fat sausages and potato fritters and all brown and crispy and what do I like best I think I like pork with stuffing I'm hungry now I really am and – oh, I must look!'

She opened her eyes suddenly before she could change her mind and there was a fraction of a second while her eyes focussed and then she was up.

'Gone! Oh, thank heaven! Thank my lucky stars!'

She turned and began to stumble off, heavily at first, tumbling, because her legs had gone numb and silly and her head still reeled. She climbed the stile and took not a backward glance at the meadow, because the fear was too strong. All the way home she sensed cats at her heels and all the way home she tried to still the refrain that ran in her head.

'They were for me! They were for me! They were for me!'

Chapter Two

It was called Half Way House, but half
way to where nobody was quite certain.
Every now and then the subject would be
brought up, and everyone would air his
theory and disagree with everyone else's,
and at the end of it all, there they would
be, back where they started – half way to
nowhere.

Ellie herself thought it meant half way
up the hill between river and sky, because
so it was, more or less. The hill was so
sheer that any view from the back windows was of living green, the sky shut
out. You saw ferns and fronds and
grasses, mint and parsley. You saw not
the branches of trees, but their knotty
roots, all within fingertip touch of the
windows. When these were opened, in

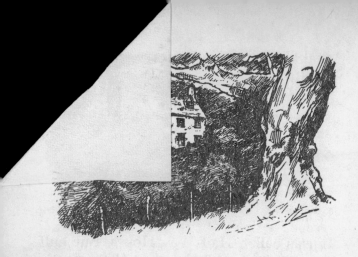

would rush a cold exciting scent of damp
earth and greenery, and you might just as
well be living out of doors. These rooms
were dim, whatever the weather, and the
very air was faintly greenish and alive.

To walk across the narrow passage into
a front room meant being dazzled, blinking and having a real shock, however many
times you had done it before. Ellie had
spent her life being startled by it. From
the windows you looked clear into space,
on eye level with the birds and striding
clouds. Away below were the wooded
slopes to the river, a glimpse of bright
water, and of the roofs of Sharlock to the
east. Over to the west, in winter when the
trees were bare, you could see the grey

walls of the tollhouse and the sturdy tower of St. Cuthbert's.

Ellie was hanging out of the window now, sniffing the early morning earthy air and searching out the meadow, half fearful of what she might see.

'No cats!'

She drew back. She had not expected to see them, but even so, the relief was so great that she was in the instant flooded with joy. She ran from the room and leapt the stairs two at a time and was in the kitchen, hugging her mother.

'Here, what's this?' Annie was knocked half sideways from her chair. She put Ellie away from her and held her by the shoulders and smiled.

'It must be that your father will come today,' she said, and her own face flushed a little.

'Oh mother – no!'

Ellie stepped back and saw her mother's face change.

'It's not that. I'm sorry, mother, I wish it was. It's something else.'

It was always Ellie who sensed which day it would be that her father would return. She would wake up one morning and be filled, for no reason at all, with a sense of delight and excitement, and would think in the instant, 'Father's coming home!'

And she would run down, just as she had done today, to tell Annie the good news. And always, before the day was out, Ellie would hear a familiar step and a whistling on the winding path up from the toll house, and race to be first to greet her father.

But he was not coming, she knew that. She felt her mother's disappointment, and herself felt sorry, almost as if it were her own fault. It wasn't, of course. She could not make things happen. All she could do was know if they would. She had known about the storm last December. There would be the bridge broken and a house blown down.

And so it had happened. The river bridge down below had been splintered and washed out to sea, and the Goodmans' house had tumbled into a ruin. Ellie had known it all beforehand. She was so used to this way of knowing, that to her it seemed ordinary, but she was coming to understand that it was not. Most people, it seemed, did not have this way of knowing things. And so she tried to hide it. She had sat shivering on the stairs in her nightdress and heard her parents talking about it.

'Getting past a joke,' she heard Annie say. 'Fancy a child that age with such terrible ideas.'

'It happens,' Fen said. 'Best not to fuss her. She'll grow out of it, happen.'

'I surely hope she does,' Annie said. 'Because I swear it frightens me, now and then. There's my own child, and sending shivers up me – her own mother. The pity is she's no brothers and sisters. Too much on her own and thinking, in my opinion.'

'No harm in thinking,' Fen said. 'Good, in fact.'

'Not good, Fen,' Annie told him. 'Not at her age. Unnatural, and maybe why she's white and skinny. There's none of the others white and skinny as she is.'

Ellie had crept away then. She lay and thought in the darkness about what had been said. She thought for a while of the brother she had never known, who had been lost when he was only a baby in The Disappearances. And she thought about herself.

'I don't think words,' she thought. 'I think pictures.'

For a long time after that night Ellie had tried not to think pictures. She did not want to be different from the ordinary. And yet she knew, knew in her very bones that with each day this power was growing stronger.

Chapter Three

The air by the river that night was chill, piercing.

'God save my cracky old bones,' Digby muttered.

He was hunched under a willow and the willow was hunched over him. His eyes glittered in the gloom. He wrung his knobbed hands, and sometimes he grumbled and sometimes he grinned.

'Worser nights than this I've watched.'

He talked to himself, and the little smoke of his own breath was all the company he could look for. Little he cared. Talk to the moon, could old Digby, to the river, the stars, the reeds – to anything. When the wind blew the reeds would even seem to answer, in faint, wordless whispers.

'Dry nights, I'm right as a biscuit.'

He watched and waited, still as stone. Anyone who could creep up close to him (and that would be one with a butterfly step, for his ears were sharp as needles) would think it time he had a wash. Time for him to dunk his tattered jacket and trews, and time for him to take a comb to his hair and beard. He was mucky, and that was a fact.

Because of his scarecrow looks and glittering eye you would probably suppose him bad. But badness and dirt do not necessarily go hand in hand, just as a double-dyed villain might soak himself every day of the year and have a hair parting straight as a Roman Road. The truth of the matter is that old Digby, like everyone else in the world, was part good and part bad. And the bad part of him included a life-long avoidance of soap and water. His wife, Tilly, sometimes got him under a tap, but he never felt right in himself for a week if she did.

Old Digby also had various skills. He could do a good imitation of a cock crow and a fairish one of a barn owl. He could catch fish, carve sticks and guess the weather, as often as not.

He was also, and most importantly, the most tireless watcher in the land of Ramazin, as his father had been before him. Tonight he was watching for The Enemy, because the old hagwitch had started her warnings again. And The Enemy, everyone knew, would come from the river. How they knew this was because it had always been said. It had been said so often and for so long that The Enemy had by now become an old friend – if anyone still believed in it any more, it was the old hagwitch and Digby himself.

Even Digby did not mean to ruin his bones for an Enemy who did not even have a face.

'Back now,' he told himself, 'and a hot noggin.'

He rose and turned his back on the darkly flowing river.

Chapter Four

The old hagwitch crooned and clucked in her dismal hut. Her fire was dim and peevish. It spat at her, and she spat back.

'Burn, stick, burn!' she hissed. But the fire was stubborn as ever. The hagwitch was not versed in the ways of light and warmth. Even her candles gutted at the least draught. Four candles she burned, but not for her own use.

That hagwitch saw in the dark as clear as in broad day, and sometimes her eyes ached when the light was bright. She kept from the sun whenever she could, and was hardly able to stand the moon when it was full. Those four candles she kept burning to north, south, east and west were not for her own use. They were meant for the world outside.

'Don't you ever forget I'm here!' she croaked. 'Don't ever forget the old hagwitch and the dark and the cold! Ice, frost and pitch black I can draw forth when I will!'

She sat and rocked back and forth, back and forth in the gloom. Only her eyes glittered, red as coals. Her skinny cat, all ribs and claws, was lying outstretched his whole lean length. The fire hissed gently.

Then there came, very faintly, the wailing.

'Hst!' hissed the old hagwitch, though there was no one to heed her. 'Hearken! 'T'is there again!'

The wailing was thin and high, the cry of a lost child, so forlorn it was, so sad beyond all comfort, that the eyes of a human would have filled with tears at the sound of it. A human would have recognized that cry as his own, as the cry of the lost child in every human heart.

But the hagwitch grinned and nodded at the sound, she hugged herself about with her skinny arms and rocked the more, back and forth, back and forth.

Outside in the dark, the voice of the lost

child wailed and wept. A shudder ran
through the very trees at the sound of it.

'Come nearer, my pretty!' quoth the old
hagwitch. 'Nearer and nearer, and soon I
shall have you!'

Already she had a thousand and more followers, the Nomen. Men they had been once, and women and children, until she had taken them with her dark powers. One by one she had stolen them over the years. Now they were Nomen, hers alone and nothing in themselves. She had them in her power to change into whatever form she pleased. She could scatter them into the air as leaves on the wind, listening spies, catching the least whisper. She could make them bird or beast. Or they could be sent out in human form, doing and speaking as any ordinary mortal. Only in this were they different – the heart of each was held by the hagwitch.

But now there was a girl in Ramazin whose power one day might threaten her own. And so the hagwitch had begun to weave snares to catch her.

'Or else,' she thought, 'she'll have my kingdom from me – Nomen and all!'

She stirred the fire with her foot and grinned.

'But never shall she have them!' crooned the old hagwitch. 'Days, nights, weeks, months, years I'll wait, century in and century out if needs be. But have that girl I will! Mine, she'll be, mine!'

They sat and hissed together, crone, cat, fire. Then, 'And the boy!' she screamed suddenly, a scream to shake the perilous flames of the candles and send shudders through the darkness beyond.

'Mine, mine, and mine alone! My slave!'

Up she sprang in a tatter of cloak and shadow. The ribby cat cowered and pressed itself near invisible. The hagwitch went stumbling into the night and knee high in wet grasses under the boughs to the rocks by the waterfall. She peered down the green shattered stairs to the cave below. Down she went, wakening echoes. When she came to the mouth of the cave, barred with iron, she paused and drew a deep breath.

'Peter!' she called. 'Peter, my pretty!'

She listened, and heard only the thin sough of wind in grass and bough blown down the stairway.

' 'T'is only me,' she coaxed. 'Your old mother. Your mistress, then, who saved your life.'

She waited for the sound of foot on stone or sight of pale face behind the bars.

Forward she went and pressed her own face close.

'There's work to do!'

Her whisper fetched echo whispers from the stones, filled the cave with the scuff of surf.

'Help your old mistress, shan't you, as you did afore?'

A great silence fell then, greater than any ordinary silence that follows a question left unanswered. And the old hag-witch clashed and chattered her teeth at her own powerlessness. Her fingers went into fists.

'Stop, then!' she screamed. 'Stop then, and starve!'

Her own words rang back at her to mock.

'Or else . . .' her voice went to whisper again, 'or else, perhaps . . . perhaps . . . you too can be changed!'

She turned then, and left the threat hanging behind her in the darkness.

Chapter Five

The place was a spotless shambles. Tilly was clean, but not tidy. Dig, of course, was neither, and never meant to be.

'The good earth's muck!' he told Tilly as she waved yet another worndown scrubbing brush inches from his nose. 'The whole world's muck – everywhere out there' – waving his arms towards the window and the general direction of the world. '*All* muck!'

'Then you'd best get out of here and *live* in the world!' She twitched her apron and glared at the trail of clods that marked Digby's latest excursion into the world. '*Not* the world, this ain't! My house, and to be kept as I like it and speckless, if you please!'

'*He* ain't speckless!' Digby gestured

now in the general direction of the rafters
of the dark room where they lived and ate
and dropped mud and scrubbed and
wrangled. 'Drops *all* sorts, he does!'

The raven flapped down past the pair of

them. He went over the table and his wings tipped a jug and there was a sudden shine in the gloom as milk spread everywhere.

'*Now* look what you've done!' Tilly screeched. 'Out my way, you dratted old fool!'

Digby was given a push that sent him staggering into a pile of turnips, onions, roots. The milk ran, the turnips rolled, Tilly scolded and the raven croaked, 'Ho, ho, ho!'

'There, my pretty,' cried Tilly, wringing milk from cloth to pail. 'Don't you be frit, my lovely bird!'

The raven shot Digby a wicked and triumphant look. He was the apple of Tilly's eye, and could do no wrong. Digby kicked at the rolling vegetables and cursed under his breath. The raven was the bane of his existence, and Digby would be within a feather of wringing his neck nearly every day of his life.

Yet the raven, Hood, was Digby's bird, and had been his father's too, and his grandfather's before that. Sometimes, when Digby felt like it, he would boast that the bird was an original exile from the Garden of Eden. This seemed unlikely to everyone, given its wicked ways.

'If that villainous bird was in paradise,' was the general opinion, 'then the Bible must've got it all wrong. It'd be him, not snake, that made all the mischief.'

'If you take me, you must take my bird,' Digby had told Tilly all those years ago. And so she had, and was a better wife to the raven than she was to himself, he reflected bitterly now as he kicked about him at random.

'Take that,' he muttered, 'and that – and that!'

A large turnip hit the fender and dislodged the fire irons with a clatter. It all but put paid to his dinner and supper as well.

'Stop it, stop it!' screamed Tilly, shaking her cloth at him and spattering him with milk. The raven, as near as a raven can, smiled.

You may wonder why Digby had not years ago put paid to this everlasting black presence in his house. The answer is that he dared not. The bird, his father had told him, would be needed when The Enemy came. And that, Digby knew, could be at any moment. He sat and scowled and harboured murderous thoughts, and did not hear the timid knocking on the door. No more did Tilly, still clattering pails and pans.

Ellie put her ear close to the door. She could hear no voices, only the rattling and banging.

'Been arguing, and sulking now,' she guessed. 'Go in or not, shall I?'

Tilly's tongue was fearsome, and Digby inclined to sulk – for hours, days on end, even. But Ellie had turned down the over-grown track to the door almost as if drawn there by a string. She had been out walking – though not in the meadow by the Braille Wood. Three days had passed without her going there again. She hardly knew where she had been walking, because she had been in a daydream, wondering what could be keeping her father away so long.

Fen was a pedlar, and as full of unac-countable ways as his pack was full of trinkets, fancies, rhymes and toys.

'It's not in a pedlar's blood to marry at all,' he had told Annie, all those years ago. 'And as to living in a house!'

In ditches, under hedges and stacks, under the moon and the weather he lay. To put a roof over Fen's head was as good as to cage a wild animal. But Annie, who had no pride because she loved Fen, and wanted to marry him, had pointed out that her house *was* nearly outdoors, on one side at least. And so Fen, when he was home, lay by the sill of a back room where if he woke in the night he could put out his head and touch fern and frond, and sniff in the strong green smells and fall back to sleep again, content.

But Annie had never been quite sure of him. She had once told Ellie that when they were first married, she would wave him off on one of his journeys and then come back in and weep into her apron, wondering whether she would see him again.

'But your coming changed all that,' she had told Ellie. ' "I've trinkets galore," he'd say, "but only one jewel." And he'd rock you for hours, and sing to you – though you'll not remember, of course.'

Strangely, Ellie thought that she did half remember nights with the air fresh on her cheek and strong arms about her, and a voice crooning. And whether or not she did, she had always felt Fen very close to her, whether or not he was away.

What she had never felt before was the uneasiness that had sent her rambling out over the fields, because she could not sit still. Fen had been gone too long, this time. Something – or someone – was keeping him. She knew it in her bones.

And like a shadow over all her thoughts lay The Disappearances. She knew that people could disappear, vanish without trace. There was scarcely a family in Ramazin who had not lost someone, over the years. As far back as living memory, and by legend long before that, there had been Disappearances. Sometimes a man might go to milk a cow or to plough his field. A woman might go to pick blackberries or glean after the harvest. They would leave their homes on a perfectly innocent, ordinary morning, and never be seen again. Children would be left motherless, fatherless – and most frightening of all, even children would vanish.

For the first time it had occurred to

Ellie that her own mother and father might vanish. And though she had vowed to try not to think in pictures again, she had been trying and trying for two days and nights now to see a picture of him where he now was.

Now her feet had brought her of their own accord to Digby's door, and she *had* to speak to him, sulks or not. He knew more than other people, and might have some answers for her, or at least some clues. Boldly she knocked again, louder this time.

'Drat!' she heard Tilly mutter. 'What gets into folks, rapping on doors when the milk's spilt? What – eeooowh!'

Her voice went up into a raw screech.

'Now look, now!' Digby was muttering.

'I *shall* look,' Ellie thought, and pushed open the door.

There in the gloom Digby and Tilly were dancing and dodging about the fire, and Tilly was all lopsided, with one foot shod and the other merely stockinged. Her shoe was in the stewpot!

She had given a kick and off it had flown – a clumsy wooden clog, made by Digby himself.

'You daft old woman!' he shouted. 'Get that mucky clog out my dinner!'

'It can *stop* there, for all I care!' she shrieked. 'All the world's muck, you said so yourself! You can *eat* muck, you can!'

The clog bobbed in the bubbling stew like a rudderless boat.

Ellie burst out laughing then – she could not help herself. She clapped a hand to her mouth to stifle the sound, but was too late. The pair of them turned and saw her and, evidently tired of abusing one another, rounded on her instead.

'*You* that bang bang banged on the door just as I was in a pickle already!'

Ellie opened her mouth to protest that she had barely more than tapped in the first place, but Tilly drew breath faster.

'*You* that made me stamp and kick and my clog to go in the pot!'

'And always bothering *me*,' grumbled Digby. 'Day and night with her everlasting who and why and what. *Now* what's she want?'

If Ellie had wanted anything less important than news, if there were any, of her father's whereabouts, she would have fled. As it was, she stood her ground.

39

'I'll fish the shoe out, if you want,' she offered. She could see that it might, in a way, be her fault it had ended up in there.

'I'm not having strangers meddling with my stews!' snapped Tilly.

'There's too many cooks spoil the broth,' said Digby unhelpfully.

'You be quiet!' she told him. 'There's all the trouble in this house comes from you!'

The three of them stood and gazed at the simmering shoe, and it seemed they might have stood there forever, mesmerized, when Tilly suddenly shrieked,

'Out it must come! Out this minute, afore it gets making my stew taste!'

She darted forward, seized a large pair of iron tongs and prodded them into the pot. But the clog was a large and slippery fish, and her face was red and wet with steam and heat before at last she landed it. It flew from the tongs and slithered on to the floor, where it lay steaming gently.

Ellie's face ached from sucking in her cheeks to stop the giggles.

'And *now* perhaps,' remarked Digby, as if the whole occurrence were the most natural thing in the world, 'I can have my dinner!'

Ignoring this suggestion, Tilly limped on her remaining clog to a nearby rocker, where she sat working it furiously. Ellie thought that if she rocked much faster she would be in serious danger of herself taking off and flying into the stew. This possibility presented such a comic picture that Ellie's cheeks finally collapsed and she burst into uncontrollable giggles.

She had a brief glimpse of outraged faces – and fled. As she went she heard a gleeful crow from the dark spectator in the rafters.

At a safe distance from the tollhouse Ellie collapsed on to the warm grass by the pathway and there she giggled herself sober.

'Oh!' she gasped. 'Oh – they're never going to *eat* it! Not now! Think of the taste! Think of the splinters!'

So taken up did she become by the matter of the exact flavour of clog-seasoned stew, that Fen was quite forgotten. When at last she did remember him, she felt guilty, as if, in some strange way, her having him in mind would ensure his safety.

She lay there, and as she gazed up at

the pale sky a sudden wave of sheer terror washed over her. So strong and so unexpected it was, that she cried out loud,

'What? Oh, what's happened?'

She saw no picture, not even a flash. She had only the utter certainty that something terrible had happened.

'Home! I must get home!'

She took the short cut through the woods. Steep steps were cut into earth and root, and away down below the river went on its long way toward the sea. The path was dark even in this bright June sunshine, she went through a tunnel of branch and greenery, and nettles stung her legs and arms.

She emerged blinking in the sudden light and there before her was Halfway House, and it looked exactly as it always had, and yet she knew that something was different. Panting, she went slowly toward it.

'Mother!' she called. And again, 'Mother!'

Silence, save for the thin whistle of birds and the faint roar of the river away down below.

'There has never been a silence like this before,' Ellie thought. 'Never.'

She passed through the door and into the echoing hall and then into the flagged kitchen. The fire was bright and crackling and she found herself faintly surprised that it should still be burning.

'A fire is, after all, alive, in a way,' she thought. And she knew in her bones that the house was empty of any human presence.

On the table lay Annie's rolling pin,

flour, butter. It seemed as if they must
have lain there for a hundred years. Ellie
felt the absence of her mother as total, it
was as if she had been made an orphan in
the twinkling of an eye. Then she wan-
dered through the house. She felt herself slow and stunned. All the familiar
objects – chairs, tables, pictures, mirrors,
seemed as if frozen, and the silence was so
dense that she could almost put out her
hand and touch it.

'Home,' she thought, 'and not my home,
now.'

The terror came again in a long, slow
hot wave. She could scarcely breathe for
it. What was she to do? Where to go? She
stood in the centre of a bare room that
looked into the sky.

And as she stood there the light
changed and the very air was suddenly
chill. Ellie hugged her arms about her and
shivered. She stared out and saw the sky
fill and darken. The light in the room grew
queerly yellowish as it did in winter when
snow was coming.

'June now ...' Ellie's very thoughts
were slow and fuddled. 'Can't snow in
June – least, not in the ordinary way of

things. Thunder clouds – must be. . . .'

As she stood, shuddering in the icy chill and staring out at the gathering skies, the snow came, in huge, papery flakes.

'No!' Ellie screamed. 'No!'

She turned and ran then, without knowing where she could run. Her frantic steps went echoing through the empty house that was darkening by the minute as the snow thickened. She ran from room to room, and from window to window, banging them fast. All she could see beyond was that dense, dizzying swirl. She could catch not even a glimpse of bright June green.

'December, is it? Time jumped on? Never! *Couldn't*!'

Ellie stood helplessly watching the snow fall. She tried to conjure up the roses in bloom beyond, the trees in full summer leaf, the long grasses. She clung desperately to this picture, as if by thinking of it long enough and hard enough she could actually re-make it, could halt that cold, relentless fall.

But the darkness grew. The snow thickened from veil to wall. Ellie, terrorstruck, cast about for a way of escape.

'Oh father!' she cried. 'Mother!'

She knew that there would be no answering voice, but she called their names again, and then again.

At last, knowing herself to be alone, she began to wail. . . .

Chapter Six

Digby was poking the fire and sighing. He had been doing it for some time: poke, rattle, sigh . . . poke, rattle, sigh. . . .

Tilly was racking her brains to remember the recipe for Granny Porter's Raisin Tart, and was not aided in the process by this succession of rattles and sighs.

'For goodness's sake, Digby!' she exclaimed at last (being undecided as to its being six ounces of treacle and three of raisins, or the other way about). 'Quit raking at that fire, will you? There'll be sparks up the chimney and the house on fire, next!'

Digby dropped the poker with a clatter and heaved a particularly deep and windy sigh.

'And quit breathing, will you?' snapped

his wife. 'How can a body think with all that puffing and blowing? Get out the house and do something useful!'

'I ain't easy, Tilly,' Digby shook his head. 'Don't feel right in myself.'

'And you'll be saying that's the fault of my stew, I suppose? Got a splinter down your gullet, did you?'

'Never such a thing,' said Digby. 'Not belly ache nor any such thing.'

'Then what?' cried Tilly, exasperated. 'Crampy legs? Cracky bones? Itchy nose?'

'I might have all of them,' he replied, 'and still be in better fettle than I am. I'm not *right* in myself, Tilly, and I'm getting nasty inklings.'

'Nasty inklings?' she repeated, deciding that the six ounces should be of treacle, and never mind if the tart was runny.

'Inklings and shivers . . .' he was talking now to himself. 'That old hagwitch has started her warnings again. And that girl, that was here just now. *She* knows. Got the sight, she has, that one, whether she knows or not, and whether she *likes* it or not. And if I'm not mistook, there's – eech!'

He let out a screech as a wet cloth

slapped down on his head and blinded him. He snatched it off in time to see the raven flap to his shadowy perch in the rafters, where beak and plumage gleamed in the gloom.

'Ha ha!' croaked the raven, and then he was in flight again, diving back and forth over Digby's head, so that he was forced to shield his face with his arms, and he cursed mightily and swatted blindly at thin air.

'Get off, get off! What – ? Let me catch you and I'll wring your neck! Leave *off*, I say!'

But Hood would not leave off. And now when he dived past Digby's head he gave a sharp prod with his wicked beak. Tilly dropped her tart-making and put her hands on her hips and rocked to and fro.

'Ha ha!' she laughed unfeelingly. 'If you could see yourself! It's as good as a play, I declare!'

Digby gave a last desperate screech and then, arms still wrapped about his head, rose from his seat and made blindly for the door. He went in a great cacophony of kicked pails, rolling saucepans and tipped-over stools. Tilly's laughter changed abruptly to screams of rage and then, with a gasp, Digby was outside and the door slammed behind him.

He lurched off up the path, leaving a dwindling trail of curses. He turned on to the road, not knowing where he was going, and kicking at stones (imagining each to be the raven). When at last he was feeling the better for this exercise and lifted his head, he was only a few yards away from the snow.

Digby's jaw dropped. He gaped and he stared. Then he rubbed his eyes with both fists, hard.

' 'T'ain't! Can't be! Snow? In *June*?'

The creamy sprays of hawthorn were all about him. The grass was long and green and scattered with daisies, dandelions, buttercups. Cuckoos called from the Braille Wood beyond. And before him was a towering wall of snow falling in great papery flakes.

'You can see the *edge* of it!'

He looked in disbelief at the clear line where the snow stopped and the summer started. It was as utterly impossible as the end of a rainbow, but there it was, but a fingertip away.

'What's happening, what's happening?' Digby jumped up and down, both knobby boots together. 'Shoo! Go away! Go away!'

He flapped his mucky hands at the unlistening snow.

'Shoo! D'you hear me? Stop it!'

At last he ran out of breath to either jump or yell, and stood gasping while slowly his brain began to work again.

'Why . . . what can it mean? That girl . . . Ellie Barker . . . was she walled in?'

Slowly, and out loud, he said, 'The Enemy. The old hagwitch. The Time has come!'

Then as he stared mesmerized at that quiet, relentless fall, the white of it was torn by a ragged black shape. It was there and gone in the blink of an eye.

'Was it . . .? Never!'

Digby went forward and took one step, then two, then another into the wall of white. He went no further, because he could not see. He held out a hand at arm's length and instantly it had gone – his arm cut off at the elbow. He snatched it back, and groped about him for the way of the maze he had got himself into. He

51

looked downwards and his boots, too, were invisible.

He whirled about and took two steps but, blind-folded by the snow, he had no idea in what direction. North, south, east and west were same and indistinguishable.

'Hallooo! Hallooo!' called out old Digby, and felt the cold taste of the snow on lips and tongue. 'I'm lost, I am! Let me out!'

He did not know whom he was addressing, nor even if there were anyone to hear. Soon his old head was silly and weak with his own spinning, and that of the snow.

'I'm not frit, I'm not!' he yelled defiantly, and that was indeed brave of him, because he vaguely knew that the old hagwitch was at work again, with her spells and ill-wishing.

Again he lifted his voice.

'I'm not frit, no, not me!'

And the words were scarcely out of his mouth when he had stumbled forward and was so dazzled by light that he flung up an arm to shield his eyes. He was back – back in June and the sunlight and the blessed green!

He stumbled to his knees, gone weak with relief. He knelt there in the warm grass while his eyes grew used to the brightness, and as the trees, the flowers, the stones of the road began to make themselves out of the blur, he saw something else.

Old Digby groaned and rubbed his eyes with his mucky hands, still wet with melted snow, so that his face was streaked with grime.

'Oh no!' he groaned. 'Can't be – 't'ain't – '*t'is*!'

They were advancing wave upon wave, tabby, tortoiseshell, ginger, black. They were in no hurry. Soft and slow-pawed they came, and stalkingly.

Digby, come straight out of an impossible blizzard to a world impossibly filled with cats, scrambled wildly to his feet. The road was still there, white and stony. He fled.

Down the road he galloped in his clumsy boots and did not stop, not even to look over his shoulder, till he was on the path to the tollhouse. Then he was inside, the door slammed behind him. He leaned against it, wheezing and blowing.

'Safe!' he thought. And then, 'Not safe. Not now. . . .'

Chapter Seven

The old hagwitch was grinning and crooning in her black abode.

'Hearken! There it is again!'

She strained her ears for the faint, desolate wailing, that seemed to come from no particular direction. It filled the air as if the whole world was full of it. It was of such despair, such grief and loneliness, that it would have melted the heart of any listener other than the hagwitch.

'Lost now, but soon to be found,' she sang. 'Nearer my pretty, nearer and nearer – and soon I'll have you!'

Her bony cat came close and rubbed by her feet but she spurned him.

'Get away!' she hissed. 'Sick of you I am, sick!'

The cat slunk off and melted into

shadow. Years long he had been companion to the hagwitch. He had sat beside her, gazing into the feeble fire until now his eyes were nearly blind, and there was no reward for his faithfulness but kicks and scoldings.

'Cats and to spare!' gloated the hagwitch. 'Where's my mirror?'

She lifted a piece of ancient glass and peered into it. At first there was nothing but a faint, smoky swirl, or a mist blown by wind. But as she stared, intent, the glass altered, lightened until it was thickly white, and she was looking at the snowstorm she had made to trap Ellie Barker in the Halfway House.

'Ah, my dearie, got you my dove,' she gloated. 'Where's a sight of your pretty face?'

In reply the mirror changed again and showed this time glass within glass – a window half veiled by falling flakes. Behind the panes was a small white face with huge, frightened eyes, looking out into a suddenly empty and altered world.

'Never you fear!' cried the hagwitch. 'Your old mother shall keep you safe, never you fear! For you're to be my darling, my daughter and the apple of my eye!'

The small white face was blank and hollow-eyed as ever. Ellie was looking out into a world made suddenly wilderness. And she did not know that a witch was watching her, spelling her, drawing her slowly into her net.

Ellie knew that she had strange powers, growing stronger by the day. But she did not suspect that one day they might equal those of the hagwitch herself. Ellie's powers, however, were of the light. The hagwitch worshipped the dark.

It would have been easy enough for the witch to rid herself of Ellie now, while her powers were new, and still growing. She could have arranged her death in a hundred different ways. Instead, she plotted to lure the girl into her own grim kingdom.

'I'll teach her new spells,' she grinned and rubbed her skinny palms. 'Spells of the dark. She'll forget the world and the light, soon enough. And she'll worship me, and be my daughter, my darling and the apple of my eye.'

For the truth was that the old hagwitch was weary of her solitude, of year in and year out with no one to give her a word, not even the boy child she had stolen from the world. She had reared him herself, he had crawled about the earthen floor with only the cat for a playmate. She had brewed for him, made gruel and broth, had carved him toys with her knobby hands.

And in those early days he had smiled at her, as babies will, had clapped his hands and laughed when she played peek-a-boo, and she thought that she had got herself a son.

But as the years passed the boy grew tall and straight and fair, he shone like a candle in that place of darkness. And some old, faint, forgotten memories began to stir, he could see in his mind's eye visions of sunlight, blossom, water shining and a wide blue sky. And he heard old remembered sounds of voices murmuring, gentle voices, and one in particular, sometimes singing. And the day came when he looked the old hagwitch fearlessly in the eye, and said,

'You are not my mother!'

The old hagwitch let out a fearful cry and clutched at her breast. She thought her heart would crack.

'How did I get here?' he demanded. 'You stole me!'

'Never!' she shrieked. 'You came of your own free will!'

Now here the hagwitch spoke truth. That baby, scarcely two years old, had come toddling out of the world and into her dark kingdom with hands out-stretched and beaming face. But it was not in greeting of the witch he came, but to pluck up the pretty stone that had been thrown into his path.

The Stone. This was the Stone whose dark powers flowed into the witch's palm whenever she wished to spell. It was her treasure, her dearest possession – that, and the Word that can never be spoken.

That day she had waited, greedy and invisible by the toll gate. She saw old Digby at work planting potatoes, and she saw the child wandering here and there along the grassy path. Digby was not used to minding children, having none of his own. And he had forgotten the danger of the toll bar. He was its keeper, but never once in his long life had it been used. It was overgrown with grass and weeds, the broken-down gate almost invisible.

All you could see beyond was a stony path, overhung with dark, fingering branches. The path was sunless. The very weather drew a line at the toll bar.

But little Peter felt no fear. He was too young to be able to conjure up pictures of what might befall him in dark places. He saw only a gate barring his way, and a rusty catch to challenge his tiny fingers. It was very stiff. Peter was not easily put off. He pushed and fiddled and rattled until his face was bright red. At last he let out the cross splutter that was his way of cursing, and let his sore fingers drop. At that moment he could have been saved, had not the hagwitch swiftly intervened.

He was about to turn in search of some more interesting pursuit, such as chasing a butterfly or prodding a snail, when something glittering caught his eye. He turned back, and peered again between the bars of the wicket.

His eyes were captured by the dazzle of the Stone. And this was no wonder, because it held an ancient and powerful magic. No human who passed into the hands of the hagwitch could be released without its touch. And nor could she herself ever set foot out of her own kingdom and into the world without it. For this reason she kept it always in a leather pouch hung at her waist.

Now, with trembling fingers, she loosened its strings and took out the Stone. She rolled it so that it came to rest just beyond the wicket.

It may be wondered why that hagwitch did not herself pass through that gate and snatch the child? The answer is that no one who had passed through that gate had ever returned. And so the catch had turned rusty with lack of use, and the path grown over with weeds and brambles.

But one of the staves was broken. It made a gap, not wide enough for the witch, but wide enough for a small child to pass through.

Now that fiercely winking Stone lay there and the child watched it greedily, and he rattled again at the catch. The witch, breath held, watched.

'Aaaah!'

Little Peter had found the gap and was through, and making straight for the Stone. Then he was snatched up and borne off, still clutching the pretty thing for which he had lost his freedom.

And so on the day when Peter, now grown tall, had accused the witch of stealing him, she spoke at least half the truth when she said he had come of his own free will.

'Tell me who I am!' he demanded. 'Where is my real mother? Who is my father?'

At first she was deaf to his pleadings, but over the years she softened, and the day came when she let him peer into her ancient glass.

When that time came Peter watched, pale and trembling. He knew nothing of

the real world except those vaguely
remembered strands of sights and sounds.
He would have prayed as he first stared
into the dark mists, had the hagwitch
ever taught him to.

Then a shape formed dimly in the glass
and he was looking for the first time at his
real home. He saw a house half way up a
steep hill, and its windows winked in the
sun and climbing flowers and ivy patterned its face. And as he stared at it he
seemed to half remember it, and slowly he
drew nearer with his longing. Then he saw
a large room, a kitchen, with rows of
shining pots and bunches of herbs hanging

from the rafters. But his gaze was on the woman who sat nursing a little girl, and that face Peter *did* know, he knew it as closely as his own heartbeat.

'My mother!'

But as he stretched out his arms the jealous witch snatched back her glass and screamed,

'No! Mine you are, mine!'

But from that moment on Peter was lost to her entirely. He turned away from her, and his looks were cold and unforgiving. He became sly. He watched carefully to see where the hagwitch hid her mirror and then, whenever he saw the chance, he would secretly take it out and gaze into it again until he made his home appear.

And so, over the years, he grew to know his father and his mother and his little sister, though he did not know their names. The glass was silent. It gave him faces, but no voices.

But he loved those faces as he could never love the hag who had stolen him away. There were long times when his father disappeared from the glass for weeks, months even. But his mother and sister were always there, and he would long to be with them, join in their smiles and laughter. He would watch until those sights were blurred by his own tears.

Sometimes the hagwitch would go off on her own.

'There's work to do – work in the world!' she told him.

And then, too, he would run to the glass and stare and stare and will it to show its other secrets. Sometimes he succeeded and the mist would clear, and he saw scenes that frightened him even though he did not understand them. He saw brief glimpses of a meadow, say, or a wood. Then he saw a man, cutting hay, or a child threading daisies.

Then the hagwitch came like a shadow in the landscape. All at once she would change her shape, and as she came she nodded and grinned and held out a skinny palm. Peter caught the flash of new gold and always, as if some ancient memory was stirred, found himself terrified, and screamed.

'No! No! Don't take it!'

Then the mists came down again and he was alone until the hagwitch came back, pleased with herself, rubbing her hands.

'Where have you been, mother?' He called her 'mother' in the hope of coaxing her secret from her.

'Never you ask, my pretty. Work in the world.'

And that was all she would ever tell him.

But as the years passed his wish to escape grew stronger and stronger. And something began to happen that was very strange. On the days when he managed to look into the witch's glass, he would very often see his sister, no longer running or playing, but sitting very still and quiet and staring into space. In the same room their mother would bake and sew and sweep, but his sister – and this was the strangest thing – would sit apart and look (or so it seemed) *straight into his own eyes*!

Could she see him – *could* she? If only she could speak – if only he could speak to her!

'Sister!' he would cry: 'Dear little sister, speak to me! Tell me at least your name!'

But she would only sit and gaze, her face solemn, even a little sad. She was as remote and separate as if they were divided by a high wall. And so they were, in a way – a wall of the hagwitch's evil making.

Despite his sister's deafness to his cries, Peter grew hopeful. In some way, he knew, she was growing closer to him. The mere feeling that their eyes were, in some strange way, meeting, gave him hope.

And then, slowly, the thought came to him that he must himself try to break down that invisible wall between them.

'Perhaps my sister is doing all she can,' he thought. 'She sits and dreams and gazes and seems to look straight into my eyes. But surely she can't see me, as I see her? She has no glass. *She simply knows that I am there*. She is doing her best – now it is up to me. I must do mine.'

Slowly, over the days and weeks and months, he began to see what he must do. His thoughts began to fix on that Stone in the witch's leather pouch. He knew that she treasured it. Sometimes, as he lay feigning sleep, she would draw it out and play with it. He would glimpse the flash and fire of it even in that dim place.

'There must be power in it,' he thought. 'That is why she loves it so, and guards it, and keeps it always about her. And so I must watch and wait, watch and wait for as long as needs be – and *steal* it from her!'

He thought very carefully how to play his game.

'I will pretend to love her again,' he decided, 'and be her son. Not too suddenly, or else she will suspect. I must be cunning – cunning as she is.'

And this is what he did. He started, first of all, to give her smiles. He sat with her in the dismal hut instead of spending all day out of doors in the woods. He could tell that she was pleased by the change in him, and slowly beginning to believe again that they could be mother and son.

Then he began to give her little things – a spoon carved out of wood, bunches of herbs he gathered. And all this time he was careful never to ask for a sight of her magic glass.

'She must think that I have forgotten about my mother and father and little sister,' he told himself.

So he and the hagwitch began to be comfortable together again – or at least, to seem so. In the evenings Peter would sit by her knee and ask her questions about the old days, and she would tell him stories, hour after hour by the sputtering fire.

Cunningly he praised and flattered her.

'How clever you are, Mother,' he told her (though that last word stuck in his throat.) 'One day, shall *I* be as clever as you? Won't you teach me? I am, after all, your son, and we should work together.'

'So we shall, so we shall,' she crooned. 'One day, I might even teach you the secret of the Stone, and the Word that must never be spoken.'

She began, then, to teach him things. At first, only little ones. She showed him how to call an owl to his hand, and how to spell the night clouds to cover the moon and stars.

'For darkness is best,' she told him. 'Remember that – darkness is best.'

Then came the day when he asked, his heart thudding,

'But what of the Stone, Mother? What of the Stone you keep in that pouch at your waist? Will you not show me its secrets?'

'Ah!' she said softly. 'The Stone. My pretty, my darling Stone. That can never be yours, my son, never till the seas run dry. Mine that is, mine! Mine till the end of time!'

'But Mother dear,' he coaxed, 'may I not even see it? I have never caught more than a glimpse of it in all these years, and I long to see it flash and glitter in your palm.'

She did not answer for a long while. Peter waited, breath held.

'A sight of it . . .' she murmured at last. 'There's no harm in a sight of it, surely?'

She unloosed the string of the leather pouch, and into it went her knobbed fingers and fetched out her greatest prize, the Stone. She opened up her skinny palm and there it lay, glittering in the gloom.

'There!' she breathed, watching it. 'There!'

And in the instant Peter's own hand went out to snatch at it, and the witch screamed and her palm shut and the cat sprang.

'So!' she spat, and the Stone was tight and safe in her blind fist.

The game was lost.

She had thrust him then into the deep cave, the dungeon, and kept him there a prisoner ever since.

And it was then that she began to have thoughts of that other child, the girl, his sister, and plot how she, too, could be drawn into her power.

'I must have the pair of them,' she thought. 'And so I shall!'

She guessed that Peter could help her in this, if he would. She waited until he had been shut away for many long days with no company but his own. Then she descended the stone steps by the waterfall and went to the barred entrance and called,

'Peter, Peter, my pretty, are you there?'

'You know I am.' His voice came dull and bitter from the shadows.

'You must be lonely,' she said. 'How you must long for the sight of a human face!'

'Not yours!' he returned. 'I can do without that forever!'

She ground her teeth in fury at this, but forced herself to go on as sweetly as she might.

'But a glimpse in the glass,' she wheedled. 'A glimpse of your little sister, far away in the world.'

There was no answer.

'Or better still,' she crooned, 'to have her here *with* you! What do you say to that?'

There was a little silence. Then she made out the pale smudge of his face as he advanced from his pitch-black corner.

'What do you mean?'

'I mean how happy you could be if we fetched your sister here,' she told him. 'How merry we could be together, all three. Wouldn't you like that? And listen, so she *could* be brought, if only you help me a little. What do you say? Think of it – your own sister!'

Silence.

'Shouldn't you like that?' she coaxed.

'Yes.' His voice was forced and grudging.

'And shall you help me?'

Another silence.

'I – I don't know.'

The old hagwitch was used to biding her time. She was used to living not minute by minute, but year by year to achieve her ends.

'Think,' she told him softly. 'Just you think on it, my dear. I'll be back for an answer when you're ready to give it.

Here's a dish of stew for you. It's hot and tasty. You should be glad I'm not so wicked as you think me, else bread and water is all you'd get.'

She left him then. Peter was left to struggle with himself in that cold place. He longed with all his heart to have his own sister with him at last. Yet how could he help the hagwitch to bring her to this terrible place?

He groaned. The hagwitch heard his groans, and smiled. . .

Chapter Eight

'*Now* you've come!' screeched Tilly in greeting. 'Now, you mucky article! Where's my bird, where?'

Digby slammed the door and leaned against it heaving for breath. He shook his head back and forth.

'Now!' he gasped. 'It's come!'

'Come? What's come, you silly old man?'

'The Time! The *Time*'s come!'

She stared at him then. Her face, red and angry, went all of a sudden pale.

'The – Time?'

Her voice was barely a whisper.

Ever since anyone could remember people had talked of 'The Time', and always with fear. 'The Time' and 'The Enemy' were terrors that cast long

74

shadows over all their lives. They seemed to be linked with the Disappearances, and *they* were real enough. No one knew when

'The Time' would be, nor what The Enemy looked like, but both were real as the air they breathed.

Digby and Tilly stood locked in a long, terrified stare.

'Out there!' Digby told her, stumbling forward. 'It's all gone mad and upside down. There's snow falling, Tilly, and a million cats!'

'Falling?' shrieked Tilly. '*Cats?*'

'Not cats, you daft old woman – snow! Snow falling. But cats coming – an army of 'em. Ooooh, I'm frit, I'm frit!'

He shook and shivered. He had watched and waited by the river at night, year in year out, whatever the weather. And now The Enemy had taken him unawares in broad daylight. He had wondered often how the Enemy would appear, but had never guessed at snow, or cats.

'Now you say it again,' Tilly ordered. 'There's *snow*, you say, in June? Where? There's none here.'

'Like a wall,' Digby told her. 'And I've been through it – more fool I. Lucky to get out again, I reckon. And what it's meant for is that girl, the one who was here and made the shoe go in the stew!'

'Her? Why her?'

'I'll tell you why,' he said, 'as I've told you before, if only you'd listened. That girl has the Sight, she sees things, knows things. And it's her brother the hagwitch took through that very wicket – or don't you remember?'

'Of course I remember!' she screeched. 'And never would that child've been taken if you'd had your wits about you! *I'd* never've let a witch take a child from under my very nose!'

'First the brother,' Digby was not really listening to her, 'and now the sister.'

They stood and nodded and stared, the pair of them. Then, 'Hood!' shrieked Tilly. 'My lovely bird! Where is he?'

'Ah,' said Digby. 'Shall I tell you? Flown into the snow, that's where he's gone!'

'And you let him? That poor, defenceless, dumb bird?'

'He ain't poor,' said Digby, 'and he ain't defenceless, and he ain't dumb. Dumb's last thing that bird is, more's the pity. *And* he's not yours, Tilly, though you like to think so. *Mine* he is, and handed down to me. And handed down for a reason. I ain't given that pesky bird house room all these years for love of his pretty ways. *Part* of it all, he is, and got a part to play. Remember, do you?'

Tilly nodded her grey untidy head.

'When The Time comes, he'll have a part to play,' she said.

'My father's very words,' agreed Digby. 'And his father's before that. And he's gone through all that snow, Till. Gone to that girl.'

'And then what?' she demanded. 'Fly off on his back, will she, through all that snow? *Very* likely!'

'That I don't know,' said Digby, 'no more than you do. But *we've* parts to play too, I daresay, and we'll do it, and do it bravely.'

'Us?' repeated Tilly. 'Why us? I don't want no mixing in with any of it. Stopping here, I am, and keep the door locked. *Cats* coming, you say?'

'An army of cats.'

'I'll fetch my broom to them!' cried Tilly. '*I'll* give 'em cats! Whose are they? They want locking up, folks that go letting cats loose by the dozen.'

'Not by the dozen, Tilly,' Digby told her. 'You ain't properly listening. Not taking it in. It'll take more than you laying about with a broom. Now sit down.'

She gaped.

'Sit!' he repeated.

Tilly, who had lived with Digby donkeys' years and had never seen him serious once, in all that time, sat. She had seen him grumbling, silly, gleeful and ratty, but never, as now, in deadly earnest. This was a new Digby, one she had never suspected. To her amazed eyes he seemed even to have changed outwardly, to be several inches taller.

'Now look,' he said, 'this is something big. It's a kind of battle, Till, and you and me to fight it.'

'But – I don't want to fight battles! I want to get my floor scrubbed and my baking done, and –'

He was shaking his head.

'No,' he said. 'This ain't an ordinary day to be doing ordinary things.'

'But I *want* to be ordinary!' she cried desperately. 'I don't want to know about snow coming down in June, and a million cats creeping up! And I won't, I won't!'

'You will,' he told her.

He *was* inches taller. He had straightened his bent shoulders under that mucky jerkin, and lifted his head.

'I'm frightened, yes I am. I can feel my heart now hammer hammer, and I want to curl up in a ball and squeeze my eyes tight shut, like I did when I was little and thought there was a bogey coming. But there's a big thing happening, Till. The biggest day of all our lives, this is. And if we don't stand up, if we don't *make* ourselves be brave, then we'll never have any more ordinary days, ever. So square up, Tilly, won't you?'

They stared into one another's eyes again, dazed by the suddenness of things, and in that silence came a clawing at the door. The latch rattled.

'The cats!' Tilly's voice was hoarse with terror. 'The cats! They're here!'

Chapter Nine

Ellie Barker, all alone in the queer snow
light and silence, was at last worn out by
weeping. She was wandering, without
even knowing why, up and down and back
and forth about the empty house,
weaving a blind invisible web.

'What shall I do?' Her mind was blank
and dazed. 'Set out into the snow?'

But the particular snow that fell in
great, silent flakes past the windows was
not December snow. She could not wrap
up well and venture into it as she might
on an ordinary winter's day. This was
impossible snow, end of the world
snow – June snow.

She felt, too, that it was snow es-
pecially meant for herself, to frighten and
confuse her, cut her off from the world.

'Mother and father – both lost!' she thought. 'And me, too, – I'm lost!'

And so she was, even in her own home, with every familiar and loved object – the pictures on the walls, the oak dresser, the worn rugs – everything all at once foreign and without comfort.

'All alone!' She drew a deep, shuddering sigh.

And yet not quite alone. This was a strange thing. Hard as she had tried of late, Ellie had not quite managed to stop the pictures that came into her mind, all unbidden. She had never spoken of it, but she had for a long time now seen the wistful face of a boy, who seemed to be trying to tell her something. These pictures had come unexpectedly, at odd moments. Perhaps as she stared into the fire his face would make itself like a pale, unlikely blossom of the coals. Or even as she helped Annie in the warm, bread-scented kitchen, his face would come silently upon the air, and she would stare helplessly back into his pleading eyes.

She had tried her hardest not to see in pictures, and yet she could not shut out this one lone face. It meant something,

she k
made it. And his sad expression
to turn he cruel – even impossible –
say someth away. He was trying to
move but cou her – she saw his lips
words.   her hear nor read the

But now, in the   snow-lit space
that had once been h ty snow-lit space
prison, Ellie too was but was now her
ened. And the thought ely and fright-
suddenly into her mind, a the boy came
first glimpse of hope.   with it, the

'He tries to *see* me,' *she* thought.
'Must – or his *face* wouldn't *come* so
often. And now, if I try to see him. . . .'

She thought no further than this. She
could not. How could she know what
might happen? It was, after all, nothing
more than a – hope.

'What I'll do,' she thought, 'I'll sit on
this stool, here, and I'll stare into the
snow. Then, when my eyes are dizzy, I'll
shut 'em – and I'll wait.'

Ellie knew that staring into snow, or into
rain, or into fire – or even into nothing –
often made pictures come. And so for a
long time now she had tried not to do any
of these things.

'And perhaps I've lo...ng.' ...ower now,'
she thought. 'For war...thought said,
Another little ec...pose, if I have.'
'And serve me righ...composed herself
But now she sa...to the window and
on a low stool fag snow. And as she
the dreamily fl...o that maze she felt a
sat and stared...ness, and without her
kind of peac...he fear left her, it slipped
even notic...And after a little time she
right away...
closed he...eyes quite easily as the most
natural hing in the world to do.

For a while she saw nothing. There was
a long, vast quiet and blank. And then,
without her so much as thinking, 'I want
to see that boy,' she saw him!

There he was, familiar as ever in a way,
with his long hair and huge dark eyes.
But now his face was altered entirely, it
was alive and dancing with joy. Straight
into her own eyes he looked and smiled,
and Ellie smiled back, knowing that he
saw her just as she saw him. (Though she
did not know that she was looking at her
own brother. She knew, of course, that
once, before she was even born, there had
been another baby, a boy. But he was

84

hardly ever spoken of. All she knew of him was he had been 'lost', and had thought that to mean 'lost forever'.)

At first she saw only his face, but then realized that, for the first time, she saw him whole – arms, legs and all. Each detail was distinct – the green of the jacket, the ragged hem of the sleeves, the bare, twitching feet. The bare, twitching, *mucky* feet. And she saw not only the full length of the boy, she saw the place he was in. There was rock, shining wet, moss, roots, earth. And beyond, struck by light from above, a flight of shattered green stairs.

It was as if it were a dungeon. But how could a dungeon contain such joy? Because the boy danced, he was wild with delight, and she saw then the glitter of his hands.

In each of them he was holding something that caught what little light there was in that dim place, and threw it off in little sparking arrows. The boy stretched both hands forward, as if to show her.

'I see! I see!' she cried, eyes still shut tight. 'But what do they mean? What am I to do?'

No sooner had she spoken the words than there was a thud, a soft but heavy thud against the window. Ellie gasped and opened her eyes.

'Oh!' she wailed. 'I've lost him now!'

She looked toward the window and saw the snow still falling but in it, half veiled, a large, shadowy shape.

Ellie screamed.

The shape loomed larger, and suddenly flung itself, like a great black glove against the panes. Ellie saw that it was a bird. It perched on the sill and rapped sharply, once, twice, thrice with its beak on the glass. Its black eyes glared straight into her own and she knew that it was asking to be let in.

'Let me in! Let me in!'

The bird had spoken.

'Impossible!' she thought. But then, so was the snow. Today it seemed that nothing was impossible.

'Silly girl!' scolded Hood – for Hood it was. 'Let me in, I tell you. I'm here to lead you.'

Ellie went to the window and opened it. A little stinging flurry of snow blew on to her face and bare arms, and in with it came the raven. She slammed the window shut again.

When she turned there was the bird, rudely making prints on the floury table and shaking his wet plumage in a spray. Ellie stood and stared at her strange visitor.

'But I know you!' she exclaimed. 'You're Digby's bird – you're Hood!'

'Nobody's bird, I ain't!' the raven snapped. 'Been waiting at his house, I have. That's all.'

'Waiting?' Ellie echoed. 'Waiting for what?'

'For The Time,' replied Hood. 'For today. And I ain't come here to chatter chatter, neither. There's great deeds to be done, and done by me and you. And mostly by me, for I'm the most marvellous and clever and noble bird in the whole entire world!'

Back and forth he strutted on Annie's table, kicking up flour as he went.

'I'm sure you are,' said Ellie humbly.

He turned and fixed her with his polished eye.

'There's no other bird I know of who can talk like me,' he said. 'Ain't you surprised to hear me talk so wise and good?'

'Yes – yes, I am,' stammered Ellie.

'I only talk because The Time has come. And there's only you for me to tell. Watched you, I have, for years and years, and you can't keep it secret from *me*!'

'Keep – what?' she faltered, though she half knew.

'The power. Power to match *hers* you have, if once I get that Stone!'

'Match – whose?'

'The hagwitch. Her for dark and you for light.'

There was a little silence.

'But haven't you come to set me free?'

'You? There's more than you need freeing,' he said. 'There's a boy, for one – and then a thousand more.'

'A boy? That boy? Him I saw again just this minute ago, and in a dungeon? Him that's kept –'

'That one,' Hood interrupted. 'You saw what he had, did you? The Stone and the glass?'

'Is that what they were? Yes, all shining and –'

'Got from that old hagwitch at last,' said the bird, and he cackled with mirth. 'She threw 'em down to him through the bars. She wanted him to help get you! And she thinks they're safe enough down there, since he can't get out. But they ain't, they ain't! Reckoned without *me*, she did.'

'I don't understand!' wailed poor Ellie. 'What about me? Stuck here in the snow – and mother and father – where are they?'

'You stop here,' the raven ordered. 'Don't you open a window or a door while I'm gone, and don't stir out a single step, no matter what! If you do, you're lost. I'm off now, to get that stone before the hagwitch snatches it back off that boy. Then it'll be your turn. Be ready!'

He launched off the table in a fog of flour and flapped to the sill. He rapped imperiously on the window with his beak.

'Open!' he ordered.

Ellie obeyed. Again she felt the cold sting of the snow. Then the window was banged to again and he was gone, a black, dissolving blur.

Ellie shook her head slowly. Whoever would have thought that hope would come in so strange and rude a shape? She had known the raven all her life, only as a noisy, bad-tempered bird in the rafters of the tollhouse. Now, it seemed, he was a kind of –

'Angel!' she said out loud, and laughed despite herself.

She pondered a while on what he had said.

'I'll shut my eyes again,' she decided. 'I'll try and see the boy again. And then, perhaps, I'll see Hood come to rescue him.'

And so she seated herself again on the stool and, as before, stared for a long time at the meandering flakes. Then she shut her eyes.

'Oh come again,' she prayed fiercely, 'do come again! I'm here, waiting for you!'

But then she heard, from what seemed a long way off, a strange, unearthly sound. It was a kind of weird music with a thousand different strands.

Ellie stiffened, then opened her eyes. If she were only dreaming, then it would be gone. But there it still was, and growing louder, coming nearer all the time. It was as if the snow itself were singing.

She ran to the window in time to see the

first of the cats combing the snow. They came sure foot and slow and as they came they made that never-before-heard music, high and sorrowful and thin drawn out.

The first of them were here now and jumping on the sills. Ellie looked right into their eyes, golden or green and all unwinking. She shrank back from their wide compelling gaze.

'They *were* for me!' she gasped.

Along the sill was a row of cats now, tabby, ginger, tortoiseshell, black. Their eyes shone like lamps and seemed to be drawing her, pulling her toward them. Their paws came scrabbling softly at the snowy glass.

'Let us in, let us in!' they seemed to sing.

She heard soft scratchings on the door, and others, fainter still, behind her.

Ellie turned and ran. She ran headlong into the back room and stopped dead. She saw a windowful of cats. They clung to the whitened roots of trees and stamped the snowy grass. She looked into a wall of eyes.

'I won't let you in!' she cried. 'I won't! Go away!'

But even as she spoke she knew, with a flash of pure terror, what their real purpose was. They had come stalking through the June winter to take her away. They were calling to her with their unearthly music, drawing her with their wide hypnotic eyes.

'No! No!'

She covered her face with her hands because she could feel herself, against her will, tempted to step out and amongst them, go wherever they went. She seemed to hear again the raven's words,

'Don't stir out a single step, no matter what. If you do – you're lost!'

Lost! She had felt herself so from the very moment she had stepped into the empty shadowless house.

'Come!' the cats mewed. 'Come with us, Ellie, come. Follow us!'

She kept her eyes tight shut and covered her ears with her hands. Still she heard them, but fainter now. Keeping her ears covered she opened her eyes, but fixed them down on the ground. Then slowly she left that room and climbed the wooden stairs to a wide room at the front of the house with windows that opened only on to space and sky. There she would be safe.

She raised her eyes and gasped. There, treading the wide stone sill, were more cats, and others swaying on the climbing roses. They mewed plaintively and Ellie, even in her terror, felt pity for them. It seemed to her that they, like herself, were lost and crying.

She went and sat on a plain wooden chair that stood in the middle of the room.

Then, hands still covering her ears, she began to sing softly an old, sad song that her father had taught her. And her own voice drowned out the music of the cats, and even gave her a kind of comfort, with the memories it brought of long-ago, safe nights by the fireside.

As she sat singing, pictures came before her eyes again. She saw a dark shape winging over a thick forest. She saw a stream in a ravine and a waterfall, and by it an outcrop of shining wet rock. And there again she saw the green, shattered stairs that led downwards to a deep cave barred with iron.

The boy was still there and held his shining prizes. He looked up and Ellie knew that he was seeing her and she smiled, even through her tears.

He smiled back, but in that very instant a crooked figure came and stood at the . bars. A skinny arm reached through but the boy shook his head and backed away into the depths of the cave.

Ellie could not hear but could only guess the scream of rage from that black, towering figure. And she guessed too that what she saw was the old hagwitch –

never seen by human eye, but by night stalking the dreams of children.

'You behave, or the old hagwitch will get you!' they were told by their mothers. Strangely, Annie had never said this to Ellie.

At the dungeon's mouth the hagwitch fumbled in her rags and drew out a key.

'She's going in! Oh – what will she do to him?'

But then another black shape came into her picture and winged down the steps to where the hagwitch struggled with the stiff lock. She seemed not to see the bird slip between the bars and make to the frightened boy. Ellie saw the flash of the Stone as it passed from palm to beak and then the raven was through the bars again as the old hagwitch clawed vainly after him and stamped her feet, and Ellie laughed aloud, with tears still streaming down her cheeks. She laughed – and in doing so she opened her eyes and lost the picture.

She was looking again at the window and the cats on the sills.

'Mustn't look at you for long,' she thought. 'Or listen, either.'

Two of the cats, she noticed, were not mewing. They stood quite still, a tabby and a large, handsome ginger, and gazed mournfully in at her.

'Specially I mustn't look at *you*,' she thought. 'Else I shall get feeling sorry for you, and let you in. Oh – how much longer must I wait here – how long?'

She closed her eyes and began to sing again, going inside herself to a place far away from the snow, and the singing cats.

Chapter Ten

'No!' screamed the hagwitch as Hood swept past her. 'No – stop thief! Come back!'

But the wings had beat past her and up to the daylight and were gone.

'My Stone! My Stone!' She clutched her breast. It was as if a dagger had pierced her heart. 'And that bird – that raven! I wish that I had struck him dead!'

Peter, crouched in the shadows of the cave, heard her cursings but could not know their meaning. He could not know that once, long long ago, that raven had been a boy like himself, one the witch had stolen and kept as her child. And when, like Peter, he had turned against her, he too had been flung into this very dungeon. And at last, when he had refused to

serve her, despite all her bribes and
coaxing, he had been turned into that
very raven that had just now stolen the
hagwitch's dearest treasure.

All those long years ago, Hood had
gone winging back into the world in his
new shape, and had chosen the tollhouse
as his dwelling. From there he could

watch the gate, there he could bide his
time, wait for his chance. He had lived
with Digby, and with his father and his
grandfather before that. He had seen
Peter, as a baby, crawling towards the
tollgate and the beckoning hagwitch
while Digby went on planting potatoes,
unaware. He had flapped and screeched

and rapped with his bill on the window, but had had nothing but a scolding from Tilly.

'You *shan't* go out,' she told him. 'Wicked pest that you are. Stop it, or I'll thump you with my broom!'

And so Hood had watched, powerless, as Peter crawled toward that shining Stone – and his doom.

But now, after his long wait, Hood's chance had come at last. The hagwitch screamed, again and again.

'You! You!' She stabbed a skinny finger at Peter and advanced toward him. 'Give back that glass – give it!'

She snatched it from his grasp and peered greedily into it.

'Show me!' she screamed. 'Give me the girl!'

The mists of the glass began to swirl, then dissolve. She saw what Peter himself had seen only minutes before. First snow, then the cats weaving under laden boughs and leaves, and among them the bright shock-heads of dandelions rearing above grass no longer green. Then, looming in that June storm, the stony face of Halfway House, decorated now with an unlikely fringe of cats.

'The girl!' gritted the hagwitch. 'Show me the girl!'

The glass obeyed. Peter, craning past the witch's shoulder, felt a pang as he saw the sister he had never known sitting forlorn in that wide room. Her white face was framed by the hands covering her ears. Her lips moved but the glass was dumb. Her song went all unheard, save by the circling cats and idle snow.

'There!' hissed the hagwitch then. 'Still in the net and trapped! But why don't she follow the pretty cats, as I meant? Ah! Eyes shut fast! *That*'s why she can't be got! You!' She turned from the glass and thrust her cruel face towards Peter's own. '*You* that's warned her of their eyes! Fool that I was to trust you with my Stone. And thanks to you, I've lost it. I'll give you thanks, if I don't get that girl. Worse than a raven I'll make of you!'

Then, clutching the glass she stared into it again.

'That bird!' she commanded. 'That raven, Hood – show me him!'

Ellie swam into the mists as the glass obeyed.

'Shall I ever see her again?' Peter thought. 'Oh, my sister – let her be kept safe! The old hagwitch may do her worst to me – but let my sister not be harmed!'

He and the witch together watched the raven's coming to the tollhouse.

'He's there!' The witch's voice held terror now. 'Quick! I'm not done yet. There are spells I can still do without that Stone. And if I don't succeed,' she turned to Peter and her cold eyes glittered, 'then I'll strike you dead before they come to fetch you!'

She stumbled from the cave, holding the glass to her breast. She slammed the gate, she turned the iron key.

Peter leaned back against the icy wall. Now he was without glass or Stone and could only guess what was happening in the world.

'There's only two things that can happen to me now,' he thought. 'Either they'll come to free me, that bird and my sister – or the hagwitch will come and strike me dead.'

He sank down to the floor of the cave, closed his eyes, and waited.

The old hagwitch went hurrying on as

fast as she was able, back to her hut to make a spell. She flapped down past the waterfall and between the boulders by the stream for all the world as if she herself were a great black bird.

But she was not used to hurrying, and her foot caught on a root, and forward she pitched to the ground. The glass flew from her grasp and down the ravine to the stream below. She heard the splinter of glass on stone.

'Oh, oh!' she moaned. She crawled on hands and knees and peered down. There she saw it, her precious mirror, all in smithereens and winking darkly.

Now, for the first time, the hagwitch knew fear. She lay panting. She felt the wet grass soaking through her robes, and her blood itself seemed to turn to water.

'They'll come, they'll come!' she cried. 'And I shan't know – I can't see them!'

For centuries the people of Ramazin had lived in fear of the hagwitch, the secret, invisible Enemy. And now the tables were turned. It was she who must wait for an invisible enemy.

She scrambled to her feet, her old bones cracking.

'Make a spell! Quick! Stop 'em, afore it's too late!'

She scurried and staggered back to her dark hut.

'Burn, fire, burn!' she shrieked, and snatched up her cauldron.

The faithful cat rubbed by her ankles, but she spurned him with her foot and cursed him.

'Out of my way!' she snarled. 'Out of my sight!'

Handsful of herbs and potions she flung into the bubbling pot.

'Now!' she muttered. 'Now – afore it's too late!'

The hagwitch could smell the cold breath of her own doom.

Chapter Eleven

Ellie still sat singing when the raven Hood returned. She opened her eyes to see him poised in the snow beyond the sill full of cats. The Stone in his beak flashed silver fire.

'You've come!'

She ran and opened the window and let in the raven and the snow together. Two cats sprang in – the tabby and the ginger that had not mewed. They came winding and purring about her.

The raven flew to the table and let the Stone fall. It blinked with an unlikely fire amongst the flour and earthen bowls.

'Quick!' commanded the raven. 'She's there spelling at this very moment. And she can see us, in that dark glass of hers. Pick up the Stone!'

Ellie advanced and first, very gingerly, touched it.

'It's warm!' she exclaimed.

'Pick it up!' Hood ordered, and she obeyed. 'And now, follow me!'

He flew from the room and down the stairs and Ellie followed blindly like a sleepwalker. He waited by the door.

'I'm to open it?' she gasped. 'To the snow, and the cats?'

'You must walk through both snow and cats,' he told her. 'But do not look to left and right. If you look into the cats' eyes for too long we are lost!'

'Oh, but – I'm frightened!'

'You have the Stone. Hold fast to the Stone.'

And so with trembling fingers she unlatched the door. Bravely she stepped into the unknown world of snow and cats.

'Follow!' she heard the raven call, and through the snow that lightly stung her eyes she could just make out the dim and ragged shape ahead.

And so the journey through that June winter began. She had barely taken a few paces before the cats were about her. It was just as she had imagined it might be that day in the meadow when she had first seen them at dewfall, coming out from the Braille Wood.

Cats were all about her, dense and urgent. So strong was their presence that she felt that she might be a cat herself. It was as if the very air were turned to fur. She tried, as the raven had ordered, to keep her eyes fixed ahead, but the cats called her and she could not resist. It was as if she herself had made them, and so she belonged to them as they belonged to her.

She looked aslant and saw them going side by side in step with her through the snow. Tabby, tortoiseshell, auburn, grey, they went in rows, neat and nice. Row upon row of pricking ears and careful paws treading the perfect snow. And as they went they sang, and Ellie was enchanted by their plaining and felt that she could follow it to the very ends of the earth. Then, first one and then another pair of clear cats' eyes turned to meet her own and even as she gazed back into them she felt as if she were drowning. Now another, now another pair, cats' eyes glowed like green and yellow lamps in the still falling snow and Ellie felt herself made heavy and powerless.

'I'll come. . . .' she murmured. 'I'll come. . . .'

But the words had hardly left her lips when she felt a sharp cuff on her head and a ragged black shape dropped between her and the eyes.

'Beware the eyes!' screeched Hood. ' 'Ware the eyes!'

Ellie came to with a jerk. She fixed her eyes straight ahead again.

'Would I, too, have become a cat if I had looked any longer into their eyes when they sang?' she wondered. 'And where would they have taken me?'

Then she was out of the snow and into the hot sunshine. She blinked and stumbled, dazzled by the sudden light.

'Safe!' she cried. 'I'm safe at last!'

Her guide alighted on a maythorn tree.

'Only saved from snow,' he warned. 'There's another journey to make now, more dangerous still. The old hagwitch will be at her spells this moment, even without the Stone. And there's these cats to be saved yet, and your own brother.'

'My brother? But –'

Ellie felt all at once weak and dizzy, she saw again in her mind's eye that boy's pale face and knew that what the raven said, although it was impossible and never dreamed of, was true.

'Taken by the hagwitch when he was a babe,' Hood said. 'That boy you saw.'

'But truly? My brother?'

Ellie laughed aloud then in sheer delight, all trace of fear was gone.

'And those cats,' the raven continued, 'they are Nomen, taken by the witch. We've them to save. We've only this one chance, else they're lost forever. And your father and mother among them. I'll be bound.'

Ellie gasped. Then she remembered the two silent cats on the sill, the ginger and the tabby, the ones who had sprung into the room when she opened the window for Hood, and wound about her feet. She turned frantically and began to scan the crowd of fur for a sign of them, but . . .

'Now, hurry!' the raven commanded. 'Follow me!'

Ellie started to run along the hot white lane to the tollhouse, and still the cats kept pace. There was no time to be lost if she were to save her brother, and Annie and Fen. She saw the raven, far ahead now, fly to the door of the tollhouse, and wondered whether Digby and Tilly were still in there, or lured away by the cats and become changed themselves?

Hood scraped on the door with his beak.

On the other side Digby and Tilly stared at one another in terror.

'The cats!' whispered Tilly.

But there was a scuffling against the window, and they turned and there was Hood, flapping and frantic.

'He's come to fetch us!' Digby's voice trembled. He threw open the door.

'Oh, my goodness' sake!' screeched Tilly, peering past him with her watery eyes. 'They *are* coming! Cats! Quick, get that door shut again!'

'They'll do you no harm,' the raven said, 'so long as you do not look into their eyes.'

The pair of them gaped. Their jaws dropped.

'You – you're talking!' Tilly accused. 'Has the whole world gone mad?'

Hood ignored her.

'That gate,' he said. 'Open it!'

'But it's not been opened for years and years. It's all overgrown, and the catch rusted.'

'Open it!' Hood ordered. 'Get an axe and smash it open, if needs be. And do it fast.'

So Digby fetched his axe and advanced toward the tollgate, knee high in grass and nettles. Tilly hobbled after him, quaking.

'We must never go through there! It's dark and dangerous! If we go through there we shall never come out again!'

Digby lifted the axe high and brought it down hard and the wood splintered. Again and again he struck, and the gate fell just as the tide of cats reached the tollhouse.

'There's that girl!' Tilly screeched. 'I *knowed* she was at the bottom of it, somehow!'

'Shush up!' Digby told her, and the pair of them stood and faced the approaching wave of cats.

'And now – follow me!' Hood said.

'We're all to go? Through that gate? Cats and all?'

The raven nodded.

'You must bring your axe. There's still work for you to do with it.'

'Then follow we shall,' said Digby stoutly. 'You catch on to my arm, Tilly, you'll be safe enough with me.'

'Oh dear, oh dear!' she wailed, but she

caught tight hold of his arm and passed with him through the broken gate and into the dark world beyond.

Ellie came close behind. Her heart thundered as she went through that forbidden gate, but she held fast on to the Stone, and conjured up the faces of her mother and father, and her long-lost brother.

They stepped from light to dark, from hot sunshine and green grass to chill mist, leafless trees and towering rocks. Ellie looked fearfully about her. The trees seemed to have a bony presence of their own, and beyond them was no sight of sky, only a low grey mist. No bird sang. They went their way in eerie silence save for the sound of foot on stone and the strong beating of the raven's wings. Their breath went up like smoke about them, even the cats made each his little smoke. There was a faint boom in the distance, as if of water falling.

On they travelled through that desolate land, and all that time the distant roaring grew louder.

'I saw that waterfall,' Ellie thought. 'It's where the dungeon is – and my brother.'

And she wondered fearfully what part she would have to play when at last they came to it.

'Shall I have to meet that hagwitch, face to face?'

She shuddered at the thought, but still kept on.

And then the cats started to sing. They lifted their voices in a song wonderfully sweet and it floated up in the misty air and reached the ears of Peter, imprisoned in his stone cell. And he wondered what creatures could make a sound so joyous in the cold land of the hagwitch, and he rose and looked through the iron bars and saw the raven who had visited him before, and taken the Stone.

'You've come!' he cried. 'Am I to be set free? Where's the hagwitch?'

'At her spells,' replied Hood. 'But spelling too late, if we hurry. We have the Stone, and now we need the Word!'

He passed through the bars and into the cave, cocking his head and with his black bead eyes darting all about.

'It was so long ago, so many ages, I can't remember!'

'Remember what?'

'I was shut up here once,' Hood told him. 'But I knew the Word, the Word that must never be spoken. And I carved it in the rock, so as not to forget it.'

Back and forth he hopped, craning and peering. And the singing cats came closer and Peter turned to see and they were there. Down the green shattered stairs they came, a procession of cats, eyes like lamps in the gloom. And there, amongst them, was the girl, his sister, though he did not know her name.

'Peter!' she cried, and they touched hands through the iron bars.

'Where's the axe?' demanded Hood. 'Break down the door, quick.'

Digby obeyed.

'Stand back!' he ordered. Once, twice, thrice, four times the axe came down on the iron lock before it yielded and the wide gate swung open.

'And now – the Stone,' Hood said. 'Bring it here to me.'

Ellie obeyed. The cats were silent now. Her footsteps rang in the hollow cave. The raven flew to her then and perched on her shoulder and spoke into her ear. Ellie looked fearfully at the rock wall.

'I am to hold the Stone, read that word carved there in the rock, then close my eyes and say it, three times, silently, in my own head. Dare I?'

She looked back and met the gaze of the thousand eyes.

She turned to face the high rock. She read that one word scratched there so long ago by a frightened boy. She closed her eyes, and held the Stone tight.

There was a queer roaring in her ears as she repeated silently the Word that must not be spoken. As the last syllable was completed her whole head seemed to fill with a clear white light.

She opened her eyes. The whole cave was bathed with that same shadowless light. As she blinked, dazzled, she was aware of the cats yawning and stretching, as if awakening from a long sleep. And then they changed, they made themselves into men, women and children, who shook their heads and rubbed their eyes, and then gave cries of astonishment and joy.

'Who are they?' She found Peter close at her side. 'And what is happening?'

'They are the Nomen, the ones who

disappeared,' said a voice. 'You might easily have become one yourself.'

Ellie turned to see another boy of about Peter's age with a bright, impudent face. He gave a mock bow.

'You don't know me without my feathers. Hood, at your service. And if I'm not wrong, there's your father and mother coming.'

'*Our* father and mother,' Ellie said to Peter.

And so they were at last united, Annie, Fen and Ellie and that long-lost son and brother. And in the very moment of their meeting there came a terrible cry from above.

They turned, then, that newborn crowd, to see the dark shape of the hagwitch towering at the head of the stairs. They saw her lift a sleeve over her eyes to shield them from the light, and then turn. She stumbled out of sight.

'Home!' The word ran about the cave and stirred the echoes.

And so the procession, led by Ellie, went up the green, shattered stairs and into the sunlight. That place was no longer the kingdom of the hagwitch, and light now struck fire from the booming waterfall and its spray. Down they went, among the wet rocks, and far below they saw the dark shape of the hagwitch in the water, as the river bore her away.

As they went the skeleton trees creaked and stretched as if released from a long cramp. The long-mute birds found faltering voice as the sun pierced through in pale shafts and the mist cleared.

Down through the forest the long procession went and Ellie led it at last through the broken tollgate. When the last of the following people had passed through, no one noticed the ribby cat that followed a little way behind. He went low, making himself flat and running from shadow to shadow, fearing a kick or a stone.

He made for the Braille Wood and stopped there till nightfall. And there the hagwitch's old cat grew fat on mice, and as time went by, made little journeys to the houses, where they gave him milk and petted him. For the first time in his life he learned to purr.

And so everyone, even the hagwitch's poor, faithful cat, lived happily ever after.

THE END

MANY HAPPY RETURNS AND OTHER STORIES
by Kathryn Cave

Alice loathes all her birthday presents on sight and finds a hilarious way of dealing with them . . .

Cousin Roderick comes to stay and causes chaos until a spider provides an unusual solution . . .

The dreaded Mrs Bannerman terrorizes her class when mystery messages from 'Billy Molloy' appear on the blackboard. Who wrote them?

And just what *are* James and Mary going to do about the dinosaur in their garden?

These are just a few of the extremely funny and perceptive stories in this new collection from Kathryn Cave, author of the highly popular *Dragonrise*.

0 552 524344

CORGI

EATING ICE CREAM WITH A WEREWOLF
by Phyllis Green

When Brad and Fat Nancy's parents go to Bermuda, they need a baby-sitter at short notice.

'Not Phoebe Hadley,' Brad pleaded. 'She almost drowned me once, and last time she baby-sat, I ended up in hospital. She always has a hobby she wants to try out on me. Please, anyone, but not Phoebe Hadley.'

But Mum and Dad were talking about Bermuda and Brad couldn't get a word in edgeways. All he could do was wait until Phoebe arrived . . .

Zany, outrageous Phoebe turned her stay into the most hilarious adventure Brad and Nancy had ever had; they never knew *what* was going to happen next! What could have caused the chicken to appear on Nancy's bed? Did they *really* eat ice cream with a werewolf?

0 552 524190

CORGI

EGBERT THE ELEPHANT
and other funny stories
by Barbara Ireson

'Who are you?' asked the mouse.
'I'm . . . I'm . . . I don't remember,' said Egbert.
'You don't remember,' said the mouse.
'I don't remember,' repeated Egbert.
'I don't remember much of anything.'

The hilarious way in which the mouse helps the little playroom elephant with his unusual problem gets this light-hearted collection off to a good start.

Other rib-tickling tales come from an array of well-known names including Norman Hunter, Beverly Cleary and Margaret Mahy.

0 552 524131

CORGI

TOM'S SAUSAGE LION
by Michael Morpurgo

It was Christmas Eve when Tom first saw the lion. His mother had sent him out to fetch logs – and there was the lion padding through the orchard with a string of sausages in its mouth! Tom couldn't believe his eyes and, worse still, when he rushed indoors to tell them, his family didn't believe him either.

There *was* a lion. Tom knew there was, knew that he hadn't dreamed it. So he sat up, night after night, waiting for the lion to return . . .

0 552 524182

CORGI

A WITCH IN TIME
by Terry Deary

'I'm running away from Harry Henson the blacksmith and his gang . . . they say I'm a witch and they want to burn me!' Ellie Nash said with a sad sniffle.

Sharon laughed softly. 'Don't be silly . . . no-one believes in witches in 1987!'

Ellie turned pale – as pale as she could under the sun-baked dust as she realized that something incredible had happened to her. Just when she was in the most terrible danger, somehow she had escaped five hundred years into the future! How had it happened? And how was she to get back?

A high-spirited adventure, packed with action and excitement, as the two girls try to solve this amazing mystery across the barriers of time.

0 552 524204

CORGI

If you would like to receive a Newsletter about our new Children's books, just fill in the coupon below with your name and address (or copy it onto a separate piece of paper if you don't want to spoil your book) and send it to:

The Children's Books Editor
Young Corgi Books
61–63 Uxbridge Road
Ealing
London W5 5SA

Please send me a Children's Newsletter:

Name ....

Address...

....

....

All Children's Books are available at your bookshop or newsagent, or can be ordered from the following address: